EARTHMEN
Bearing Gifts

EARTHMEN
Bearing Gifts
FREDRIC BROWN

ÆGYPAN PRESS

Special thanks to Greg Weeks, David Wilson, and the Online
Distributed Proofreading Team (which can be found at
http://www.pgdp.net).

This story was first published in the June, 1960, issue of
Galaxy magazine.

Earthmen Bearing Gifts
A publication of
ÆGYPAN PRESS

www.aegypan.com

Mars had gifts to offer, and Earth had much in return — if delivery could be arranged!

*D*har Ry sat alone in his room, meditating. From outside the door he caught a thought wave equivalent to a knock, and, glancing at the door, he willed it to slide open.

It opened. "Enter, my friend," he said. He could have projected the idea telepathically; but with only two persons present, speech was more polite.

Ejon Khee entered. "You are up late tonight, my leader," he said.

"Yes, Khee. Within an hour the Earth rocket is due to land, and I wish to see it. Yes, I know, it will land a thousand miles away, if their calculations are correct. Beyond the horizon. But if it lands even twice that far the flash of the atomic explosion should be visible. And

I have waited long for first contact. For even though no Earthman will be on that rocket, it will still be first contact — for them. Of course our telepath teams have been reading their thoughts for many centuries, but — this will be the first *physical* contact between Mars and Earth."

Khee made himself comfortable on one of the low chairs. "True," he said. "I have not followed recent reports too closely, though. Why are they using an atomic warhead? I know they suppose our planet is uninhabited, but still —"

"They will watch the flash through their lunar telescopes and get a — what do they call it? — a spectroscopic analysis. That will tell them more than they know now (or think they know; much of it is erroneous) about the atmosphere of our planet and the composition of its surface. It is — call it a sighting shot, Khee. They'll be here in person within a few oppositions. And then —"

Mars was holding out, waiting for Earth to come. What was left of Mars, that is; this one small city of about nine hundred beings. The civilization of Mars was older than that of Earth, but it was a dying one. This was what remained of it: one city, nine hundred people. They were waiting for Earth to make contact, for a selfish reason and for an unselfish one.

Martian civilization had developed in a quite different direction from that of Earth. It had developed no important knowledge of the physical sciences, no technology. But it had developed social sciences to the point where there had not been a single crime, let alone a war, on Mars for fifty thousand years. And it had developed fully the parapsychological sciences of the mind, which Earth was just beginning to discover.

Mars could teach Earth much. How to avoid crime and war to begin with. Beyond those simple things lay telepathy, telekinesis, empathy. . . .

And Earth would, Mars hoped, teach them something even more valuable to Mars: how, by science and technology — which it was too late for Mars to develop now, even if they had the type of minds which would enable them to develop these things — to restore and rehabilitate a dying planet, so that an otherwise dying race might live and multiply again.

Each planet would gain greatly, and neither would lose.

And tonight was the night when Earth would make its first sighting shot. Its next shot, a rocket containing Earthmen, or at least an Earthman, would be at the next opposition, two Earth years, or roughly four Martian years, hence. The Martians knew this, because their teams of telepaths were able to catch at least some of the thoughts of Earthmen, enough to know their plans. Unfortunately, at that distance, the connection was one-way. Mars could not ask Earth to hurry its program. Or tell Earth scientists the facts about Mars' composition and atmosphere which would have made this preliminary shot unnecessary.

Tonight Ry, the leader (as nearly as the Martian word can be translated), and Khee, his administrative assistant and closest friend, sat and meditated together until the time was near. Then they drank a toast to the future — in a beverage based on menthol, which had the same effect on Martians as alcohol on Earthmen — and climbed to the roof of the building in which they had been sitting. They watched toward the north, where the rocket should land. The stars shone brilliantly and unwinkingly through the atmosphere.

*I*n Observatory No. 1 on Earth's moon, Rog Everett, his eye at the eyepiece of the spotter scope, said triumphantly, "Thar she blew, Willie. And now, as soon as the films are developed, we'll know the score on that old planet Mars." He straightened up — there'd be no more to see now — and he and Willie Sanger shook hands solemnly. It was an historical occasion.

"Hope it didn't kill anybody. Any Martians, that is. Rog, did it hit dead center in Syrtis Major?"

"Near as matters. I'd say it was maybe a thousand miles off, to the south. And that's damn close on a fifty-million-mile shot. Willie, do you really think there are any Martians?"

Willie thought a second and then said, "No."

He was right.

— FREDRIC BROWN